Darren Dwayne DeBakey
— and —
His Amazing Inventions

Written by Teresa Turner
Illustrated by Jack Pittman

STECK-VAUGHN
A Harcourt Company

www.steck-vaughn.com

Contents

Chapter One
The Most Boring Summer Ever

Darren Dwayne DeBakey blinked and stared at the ceiling above his bed. He was having the dullest summer he could remember. Sighing heavily, he plodded downstairs and put some bread in the toaster. When the toast popped up, it was slightly burned. Darren sat down at the table and set the toast in the automatic toast scraper he had invented. The scraper took off the black part.

Darren's father was using Darren's first invention, the hands-free hanging newspaper rack. The rack hung down in front of Darren's father's chair. Clips on its four corners held the newspaper in place. "Are you going to invent something today?" Darren's father asked.

"I'm all out of ideas," Darren said sadly.

After breakfast Darren decided to take a bike ride. As he went out the front door, he pressed the howling doorbell he had invented. It sounded just like a wolf. Inventing the doorbell had been fun. Darren wished he could think of something else to invent.

Outside, Darren rode his bike past the basketball court at school. Patrice, J.W., and Joanna were shooting baskets. "Come play with us!" they called.

"No, thanks," Darren replied and pedaled on. As he rode past the fire station, he saw that Mr. Ramirez and Ms. Lee were washing the fire truck.

"Hi, Darren!" they called. "Do you want to help us wash the truck?"

"No, thanks," replied Darren.

As he topped a hill, he noticed the library. *Maybe I can find something to read,* he thought. He parked his bicycle and went in.

"Good morning, Darren," said Mr. Goggans, the librarian.

"Good morning," Darren said.

"Can I help you?" Mr. Goggans asked.

"No, thanks," answered Darren.

Chapter Two
A Very Strange Book

Starting at the front of the library, Darren walked slowly through the children's section. On one of the fiction shelves, he noticed *The Adventures of Dusty Dirk, Cowboy*. Darren had already read it. He pulled *Time Stands Still* off the shelf and looked at it. Then he put it back. His fingers rested on *Race to the Finish*. Darren wrinkled his brow and frowned. That wasn't what he wanted to read either. He moved on to the nonfiction. He could read about volcanoes, deep-sea fishing, wild cats, or life in the Wild West. Somehow nothing sounded interesting.

Darren wandered out of the children's section and into the books for grown-ups. Winding through the rows of shelves, he found himself at the very back of the library, where the lights were dim. Darren looked at the titles on the shelves in front of him. He pulled out *Learn Spanish the Easy Way* and then put it back.

He thumbed through *Gardening Made Simple* and slid
it back onto the shelf, too. Then, on the very top shelf,
Darren spied a beautiful book bound in bright red
leather. Fancy designs in real gold ran down the spine.

Darren found a stool and reached up for the book.
It was still too high. Darren stood on his toes and
stretched as high as he could. With the tips of his
fingers, Darren inched the book off the shelf. Then he
jumped off the stool and sat on the floor. Carefully
opening the book, he turned the first page to read the
title, written in curvy letters: *My Travels to Other
Dimensions by Sir Dagobert Ignatius LaFleur.* On the

facing page was a picture of a man. He had a long nose, a huge mustache, and a three-cornered hat with a big feather.

I wonder what he means by other dimensions, Darren said to himself. He turned the page. At the top of the next page, the book said, "What I Mean by Other Dimensions." Darren read on:

> When I use the word *dimensions,* I mean "worlds." The world in which you live, dear reader, is a dimension. The universe contains millions of dimensions stacked up like layers in a cake. You cannot see the other dimensions, and the beings in them cannot see yours. Yet I, Sir Dagobert Ignatius LaFleur, have found a way to travel between dimensions.

Darren could hardly believe the paragraph he had just read. He thought about how exciting it would be to go to other worlds. *I wonder if I can travel to other dimensions,* Darren thought. He turned the page. The first chapter was titled "How You, Too, Can Travel to Other Dimensions."

Darren read and read, even though LaFleur's book was hard for him to understand. Complicated charts and diagrams filled the chapters. Long number sentences with strange symbols danced across the pages. Darren was so interested in what he was reading that he didn't feel his eyelids growing heavier and heavier.

"Darren! Darren DeBakey!"

Darren's eyelids snapped open.

"It's six o'clock," Mr. Goggans called. "Time to close!"

"I'm coming!" Darren called. He climbed on the stool and put the book back in its place. Then he got on his bike and headed home.

Darren's mother was standing in the front door. "Where were you all day?" she asked with a frown.

"I was at the library. I fell asleep reading. I'm sorry I worried you."

"All right. But next time, let me know where you're going before you leave the house."

That night Darren dreamed he was a famous scientist. He had a huge lab full of all kinds of equipment. People came to shake his hand. He had invented a machine for traveling to other dimensions.

Chapter Three
The Best Invention Yet

Early the next morning, Darren jumped out of bed. He ran down to the basement, where he kept all his spare parts. He had two old television antennas, three wind-up clocks, a broken electric toothbrush, an old battery-powered radio, and a big box full of wires and gears.

Darren sat at a dusty card table and looked through his books about time, space, energy, and motion. Then he drew some diagrams.

ATTACH TO BIKE

TIMER

TUNER

TUNER

SWITCH →

BATTERIES

Darren's mother came down the stairs with a bowl of oatmeal. Darren's baby sister followed her. "What are you inventing this time?" his mother asked with a smile.

"It's a secret," Darren said.

His mother put the bowl of oatmeal on the table.

"Thanks, Mother," he said.

Darren's mother went back upstairs, but his baby sister, Annabel, stayed. Darren kept an eye on her. She played happily with odds and ends from the box. She handed Darren the things he needed: an old clock, the radio receiver from the old stereo, some batteries, and the television antennas.

Darren worked throughout the morning. At lunch his father brought him a sandwich. Darren kept working. This was the hardest thing he had ever tried to invent. Finally Darren was finished. The radio was wired below the clock's face. Two antennas stuck out of the top of the clock. Darren carried his invention upstairs. "I'm going for a ride," he told his mother.

"It had better be a quick one," his mother said. "It's almost time for dinner."

Using some heavy-duty tape, Darren attached his invention to his bike. He turned on the radio and fiddled with the radio dial. The radio made a whining sound. Next, Darren adjusted the antennas until the sound went away. Finally, he set the clock hands to six o'clock. Then he got on his bike and rode to Ervay Street, which was long and straight and downhill.

As he started down Ervay, he pedaled until his legs were a blur. Faster and faster he flew, and then the edges of everything around him began to turn pink. A strong wind circled around him, making his stomach feel queasy. The wind picked up speed and whirled faster and faster until the streets, the houses, and even the people turned deep red. Then everything went fuzzy at the edges, turned purple, and disappeared. A sound like the unzipping of a giant zipper ripped through Darren's head. Darren blinked his eyes and opened them wide. He was in a very strange place.

Chapter Four
A Place Called Greater Floundermuffin

Darren stopped pedaling. He stood on a large, flat, paved space. At first the people walking around looked normal to him. Then he noticed that their hair was sticking straight up. As he studied the people more closely, he saw that everyone, even the children, carried walking sticks. Darren was so busy looking that he didn't notice that he and his bicycle had floated up into the air. Darren tried to stretch his toes to the ground, but he just floated higher. From his overhead view, Darren could see big square holes in the concrete. Each hole held a staircase leading down. *Where do those stairs go?* Darren wondered. *And why am I floating?*

Just then a girl who looked his age marched up to him. She was wearing purple tights with a green-and-blue checked dress. Her three pigtails stood straight up on her head. She had a walking stick in each hand. "Where's your groundermajig?" she asked.

"My what?"

"Here," said the girl. She pushed a red button on one of the walking sticks. Then she handed the walking stick up to Darren.

Darren looked at the walking stick. It was thick and heavy, and it had a round handle on the top. At the bottom it was open. Little wheels surrounded the opening.

"Turn it on," said the girl.

Darren pressed the red button. He drifted gently down to the pavement.

"Thanks," said Darren. "I'm Darren Dwayne DeBakey. I'm new around here."

"No kidding," said the girl. "I'm Thompson Erika. I think you'd better go by DeBakey. Darren is a weird first name."

Darren felt a cool breeze on his stomach. He looked down to see his shirt climbing rapidly up his middle. The legs of his jeans were working their way up toward his knees, too.

Thompson Erika sighed. "I see you don't have any downingwings either. I'll lend you one." She unclipped something from the hem of her dress and handed it to Darren.

It was a clip with small golden wings like a moth's. Darren fastened the clip onto the hem of his shirt. The little golden wings started beating. The clip flew toward the ground. Slowly the front of Darren's shirt straightened.

"How does this stuff work?" Darren asked.

Thompson Erika wrinkled her forehead and studied Darren. "Don't they have schools where you come from?"

"We have schools. It's just that everything is different where I come from. There, gravity pulls us toward the ground. We don't need groundingwings or downermajigs, or whatever you call them."

"Gravity pulls you *down?*" Thompson Erika asked. "I'll believe it when I see it."

"Are you going to tell me how these gadgets work?"

"The groundermajig has a little motor that creates suction. The suction pulls you down to the ground. The downingwings have a tiny battery in them. It makes the wings beat."

"That's excellent!"

Thompson shrugged. "I guess so."

Chapter Five
A Floundermuffin Friend

While Darren and Thompson were talking, a machine rolled up to them. It was about the size of a small refrigerator. The middle had a big square flap that looked like a mouth.

"Would you like something to drink?" it asked.

Darren's mouth dropped open.

"What do you have?" Thompson asked.

"Pickle juice, sauerkraut juice, and beet juice."

"Not for me, thanks," Thompson said. "What about you, DeBakey?"

Darren thought the drinks sounded awful. Still, he wanted to see how the invention worked. "I'd like some pickle juice, please."

"Ten zlots, please."

Darren dug all his change out of his pocket.

"Is that money?" Thompson asked.

"Sure." The coins floated above Darren's hand.

"Here, I'll trade you." Thompson plucked a nickel out of the air and gave Darren a little square piece of plastic. "Put it in the flap."

Darren reached his hand into the machine's flap and let go of the plastic square.

"Stand back," said Thompson.

A mechanical arm shot out of the top of the machine. It was holding a plastic cup upside down. Below it was a little faucet. The faucet shot a stream of pickle juice straight up into the cup. When it was done, Darren took the cup. It was still upside down. "How do I drink it?" Darren asked.

The mechanical arm retreated and came back out holding a U-shaped straw. Darren took it and sipped the salty pickle juice. "What a cool invention!" he exclaimed. "This is the most interesting place I've ever been."

"Interesting?" repeated Thompson. "You must be kidding. There's nothing interesting in Greater Floundermuffin. Come with me, and I'll prove it."

"Greater Floundermuffin?" Darren asked.

"That's where you are," Thompson explained. "You're in Greater Floundermuffin, the dullest place in the world."

Thompson walked off and Darren followed until he remembered that his bike was still floating in the air. "Hey wait! My bike!" he cried.

Thompson took the red ribbon off the end of her middle braid. She tied one end to the bike's front wheel. Then she handed Darren the other end. Off they went, the bike floating behind them like a balloon.

"First," Thompson said, "I'll take you to the park." Thompson led Darren to one of the square holes. She pointed to a metal ring attached to the concrete.

"You can tie your machine up here," she told Darren.

Darren tied his bike to the ring. Thompson started down the stairs.

"I thought we were going to the park," said Darren.

"We are," said Thompson.

"There's a park under the ground?" Darren asked.

"Where else?" said Thompson.

Thompson and Darren went down the staircase. At the bottom stood a shiny metal wall. Darren couldn't see any door.

"Please let me in," Thompson said very politely.

Nothing happened. Thompson turned to Darren. "You have to ask, too."

"Let me in," Darren said. Still nothing happened.

"You have to ask like you *really* want in."

Darren felt very silly. "Please, please let me in," he said. The metal wall silently slid up. Thompson and Darren went in only to face another shiny metal wall. The door they had just passed through slid closed. *We're trapped!* Darren thought.

"If it's not too much trouble, could you please let us in?" Thompson said to the wall. She turned and looked at Darren.

"We would really appreciate it if you would let us in," he said.

The wall slid to the left. When Darren stepped inside, he felt the back of his shirt fall down. His jeans slid back down his legs. "Hey," he said, "gravity's pulling me down!"

"Sure," said Thompson. "All our buildings have gravity-reversing machines."

They were in the strangest park Darren had ever seen. It was as big as a football field. The ceiling looked like rock, and the floor and the walls were dirt. Lamps on the walls and ceiling gave out a dim light. Paths covered with gravel wandered between clumps of strange plants. Darren looked more closely. They weren't plants at all. They were mushrooms! Some were the size of buttons, and others were the size of trees. There were mushrooms shaped like shoes and mushrooms shaped like boats. "They're beautiful!" said Darren.

Thompson shrugged. "I guess," she said.

Darren walked down all the paths. Thompson followed him, yawning. "Come on," she said. "Let's go to the museum."

The steps down to the museum were made of shiny green stone. The doors looked like pure gold. "You have to be extra polite to the museum doors," Thompson whispered. She looked at the door and smiled. "Please, if it's not too much trouble, do you think you could let us in?"

Darren cleared his throat. "I hate to bother you," he began. He felt very foolish. "If you're not busy right now, I would be very grateful if you would let me in."

The door slid open to reveal a little room with a shiny green floor and walls. On the wall facing Darren and Thompson, gold letters spelled out "The Greater Floundermuffin Museum of Inventions." Darren and Thompson went through a door on their left.

They found themselves in a big white room lined with strange objects. In the middle of the room floated a statue of a man. "This is Contumacious Carl's room," Thompson told Darren. "He lived a long time ago. Back then, people didn't even have first names."

"What does *contumacious* mean?" Darren asked.

"It means 'hard to get along with.' He was a brilliant inventor, though."

Darren walked up to the statue. He waved his hand under it. There was only air. He looked at the statue's head, but he couldn't see any wires holding it up. "Okay, I give up," he said. "How does it do that?"

"Do what?" Thompson asked.

"Hang in the air like that."

"There's a powerful magnet inside the statue," she explained. "More magnets are hidden in the ceiling and the floor. The one in the ceiling pushes the statue down, and the one in the floor pushes it up."

"Amazing!" exclaimed Darren.

"Not really," said Thompson.

Darren examined the statue. The man's trousers had one long leg and one short one. Likewise, his shirt had one long sleeve and one short one. He also wore an odd hat. Darren stood on his tiptoes to see it better. It was shaped like a big flat fish! "Hey, Thompson!" Darren called. "Why is Carl wearing a fish on his head?"

"The climate was much colder then, so they wore flounders to keep their heads warm."

Darren wondered whether Thompson was pulling his leg. She looked very serious. Darren went over to a big, complicated invention. Part of it looked like an oven on tall legs. Holes in the bottom of the oven drained into a chute. The chute emptied into a cauldron. A twisting copper tube came out of one side of the cauldron. It emptied into a shallow pan. "What on earth does this invention do?" Darren asked.

"It turns gold into plastic," Thompson answered.

Darren started to ask why anyone would want to do that. Then he remembered that Floundermuffin money was made of plastic. "Does it work?" he asked.

"It used to," said Thompson. "It made Carl a very rich man."

"Why doesn't it work any more?"

"Carl refused to tell anyone the secret ingredient that he added to the gold," Thompson answered.

Darren walked over to another invention. The bottom part of the invention looked simple enough. It was just a wooden handcart. Out of the top of the handcart, though, snaked a dozen very long, flexible metal tubes. Each one ended in a mechanical hand. Darren studied the hands and saw that some of them held little pairs of clippers. "Okay," said Darren. "I

give up. What does this do?"

"It used to pick grapes," Thompson said, "but Carl destroyed the engine before he died." She opened a door in the side of the cart. "See? It's empty."

Against another wall stood something that looked like a wooden boat with large canvas wings. "This is Contumacious Carl's ferret-powered flying car," she explained. "The wings are attached to the ferret wheel."

Darren leaned over the edge of the car. In the middle was a little treadmill. "I don't suppose this contraption worked," said Darren.

Thompson yawned. "No one knows," she said. "Carl had a patent on it. The patent says that no one can ever build one except Carl."

"Why would Carl want to keep other people from using his inventions?" Darren asked.

Thompson sighed. "Because he was hard to get along with. That's why he was called Contumacious Carl. Come on, let's do something else."

Reluctantly, Darren agreed. When they got back up to the ground, his stomach growled. He untied his bike wearily. He was just about to ask Thompson if they could get a snack when he heard a terrible scream.

"What is that horrible noise?" Darren asked Thompson as he looked around.

"That's the clock. It's almost time for dinner. Do you want to come home with me?"

"Do you mean the clock screamed?"

"I guess you're going to tell me that where you're from, clocks don't scream. So, do you want to have dinner at my house?"

"Um, sure. Can we see the screaming clock first?" asked Darren.

"We can if we hurry," said Thompson.

They walked as fast as they could, and soon Darren saw an hourglass standing on a street corner. The top part of the hourglass was empty. Fuzzy balls like tennis balls floated inside the bottom part.

A pole stuck out from the middle of the hourglass. Attached to the pole was a statue of a woman. It looked like the statues in the museum except that its mouth was open. Between its hands the statue held a sign. The sign showed a picture of a family sitting down for dinner.

"You see the picture?" said Thompson. "That means it's the dinner hour."

Darren stared at the clock as it screamed again. "How does it work?" he asked Thompson.

Thompson sighed. "When all the balls are in the top, the clock turns over. When it turns, it makes the woman scream and changes the picture on the sign."

"Yes, but how?" Darren asked.

"Beats me," said Thompson. "Maybe later you can ask my mother. She'll know."

Thompson jogged away and Darren followed her. They jogged for a long time, and Darren ran out of breath.

"You sound worn out," said Thompson. "We'd better catch a sail taxi." She looked up and held her arm high in the air.

Darren looked up, too. He saw a giant purple and orange kite swoop down. As it came closer, Darren could see a man strapped in the middle of the kite. He was holding a giant groundermajig, and it was pulling the kite down to the ground. It stopped right in front of Darren and Thompson. Darren saw a harness on each side of the man.

"Tie your bike to the tail," he said. Darren tied his bike tightly. "Now hop aboard!"

Darren and Thompson slipped into the empty harnesses and tightened the seat belts around their waist. Darren noticed a rope attached to the kite.

The man pointed a remote control, and Darren saw a strange invention shaped like a small suitcase with wheels. The kite's rope was tied to a handle on its back. The man turned off his giant groundermajig and they began to float. Then he pressed a button, and the machine raced over the concrete. The rope straightened, and the kite began to move.

"Where to?" asked the man.

"The Outer Burgs, please," Thompson answered.

"How does that machine down there work?" Darren asked.

"You mean the engine?" asked the taxi driver. "It runs on solar power. The sides collect the sun's energy. The energy drives the wheels."

"But why doesn't it float?" asked Darren.

"It has a groundermajig in the middle, of course," said the taxi driver. "You must not be from around here," he said. "Everyone in Floundermuffin knows that."

Chapter Six
Broccoli Ice Cream and Pet Worms

Darren was sorry when he and Thompson reached the end of their ride. Flying was fun.

"Come on," said Thompson. "We don't want to be late for dinner." They ran past one hole after another. "Here we are!" she finally said. They tied up Darren's bike and dashed down the stairs. "Open up!" she said to the door. Darren guessed that people didn't have to be polite to their own doors.

Inside the Erikas' home, Darren watched Thompson put her groundermajig in a little pail that looked like an umbrella stand. He did the same.

Thompson's mother was already sitting down at the dining room table. "Here you are, just in time!" she said when Thompson and Darren hurried into the room.

"Mother, this is DeBakey," said Thompson. "Can he have dinner with us?"

"As long as it's all right with his parents," said Thompson's mother.

"It's fine with them," replied Thompson quickly.

Thompson and Darren sat down. Thompson's mother called into the kitchen. "There will be one more for dinner, dear!"

In a moment Thompson's father came out of the kitchen with a tray. "Here's the first course!" he announced and set steaming bowls of soup down in front of them. Darren sipped a little soup from his spoon. It tasted like hot lime gelatin. Darren decided to wait and see what else they were having.

Thompson's father brought in the second course. "I made your favorite," he said to Thompson. "Iced chicken with pumpkin-raisin sauce."

Darren looked at it. He took a nibble. It was awful. He pushed his chicken around on the plate so that it would look like he had eaten some of it.

"Is everyone ready for ice cream?" asked Thompson's father.

"Yes, please!" said Darren. *Finally!* he thought. *Something I can eat!*

But when Darren got his dish of ice cream, it was full of green chunks. He dug one out with his spoon. It was broccoli! Darren sat and watched his ice cream melt, glad that no one was noticing he was not eating anything.

After dinner Thompson asked Darren if he wanted to see her worms. Darren's stomach felt queasy, but he wanted to be polite. "Sure," he said.

Thompson took Darren to a musty little room filled with tanks and tanks of dirt. Some were big, and some were small. They were all full of nasty, slimy worms.

"I have more worms than anyone else at my school," Thompson said proudly.

"Cool," said Darren weakly.

Thompson took the top off of a small tank. "These are my racing worms," she told Darren.

When the worms heard Thompson's voice, they all came wriggling out of their holes. They were long, skinny, green worms with orange heads. Thompson put her finger down in the tank. One of the worms crawled onto her finger. She lifted it like a piece of spaghetti and then draped it over her palm. "This is Lightning," she said. "He won the Division Two title last year."

"Oh," said Darren, who had begun to look a little green himself.

Thompson took Lightning to a table. On top of the table lay a long box of dirt with a little oval track in it. A piece of ribbon marked the finish line. Thompson put Lightning down at the start of the race course, picked up a tiny green flag, and waved it in front of Lightning. "Go!" she said.

Lightning took off. When he passed the finish line, he stopped. "Good worm!" said Thompson.

"That's the fastest worm I've ever seen," Darren said, trying not to look at it.

Thompson smiled. She put Lightning back in his tank. "Over here," she said, "are my horned worms. They glow in the dark."

"Hmm," said Darren, holding his stomach.

Thompson switched off the light. The worms gave off a yellow glow. Thompson picked up a big handful of them. "Do you want to hold them?" Thompson asked.

"No, thanks," Darren quickly answered.

Thompson put the worms back in their tank and turned on the light. "This one is my favorite," she said, pointing to a slime-covered tank. "It's a Martian oozing slug. I had to save up my allowance for six months to buy it, but it was worth every zlot."

Feeling very dizzy, Darren followed Thompson to a small tank that held a pale yellow worm with purple spots. As Thompson reached in to get the worm, she brushed her hand against the slime on the 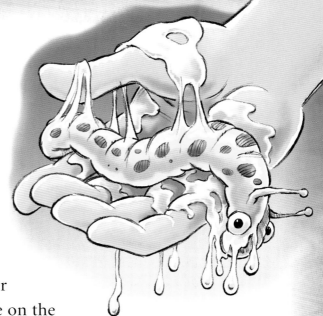 tank. Darren's stomach heaved, and his skin began to crawl as he watched the short, fat worm cover itself with slime.

With a mighty effort, Darren swallowed hard to keep himself from throwing up. "It's really interesting," he said to Thompson, "but it's getting late. I should go home."

"But you haven't seen all my worms."

"Maybe I could come back another time," said Darren. "My parents will be worried."

Darren thanked Thompson's parents for dinner. Then he and Thompson went up the stairs and untied Darren's bike. It was dusk.

Thompson held Darren's bike while he turned on the radio receiver and fiddled with the antennas. He turned the clock back to six o'clock. Then he climbed on his bike and handed his groundermajig to Thompson. As he began to float upward, he waved to her. "Goodbye, Thompson Erika," he said.

"Goodbye, DeBakey. Come back soon."

Darren started to pedal. It felt very strange to pedal in midair. Soon everything turned purple. The wind came up, and then everything went fuzzy around the edges and turned red. Finally Greater Floundermuffin turned pink and disappeared. The loud zipping noise echoed through Darren's head.

BAM! Darren's front tire hit the ground hard. Darren looked around and breathed a sigh of relief. Here was his street, and it was still light outside! As Darren rode by the basketball court, Patrice made a perfect jump shot. Finally Darren saw his own front door. He jumped off his bike and ran inside. His mother was in the kitchen. Darren gave her a big hug. His father was playing with Annabel. Darren hugged him, too. Then he picked up his baby sister. He wondered how long he had been gone.

"Dinner's ready!" Darren's mother called. She had been starting dinner when Darren left. He had only been gone a few minutes! Darren sat down at the table. His mother brought out roast beef and green beans and sweet potatoes. Darren ate until he couldn't hold another bite.

That night Darren snuggled into his own bed. He dreamed of all the dimensions he could visit with his amazing invention.

Chapter Seven
Home to Stay?

Darren slept late the next morning and woke up wearing a big grin. He was the only person in the whole world who could travel to other dimensions. Then Darren remembered that he had left his invention outside on his bike. He raced downstairs and dashed outside to get it. His bike lay on the ground. Where his invention should have been, there was nothing!

Darren looked all around the front yard. Then he looked in the basement. He looked in the living room, where Annabel sat in the middle of the floor. She was playing with something. As Darren walked closer, he spied the clock lying in bits and pieces on the floor. "Oh, Annabel!" he cried.

Annabel held out a bent antenna for him to see.

Darren stared at his broken invention. He felt like crying when he remembered he had almost no spare parts to use to make another one. Then he thought of

LaFleur's book. *I'll make another kind of dimension machine!* he told himself happily. *All I have to do is look in LaFleur's book.*

Darren jumped on his bike and rode to the library. Inside, he walked quickly to the shelf where he had found LaFleur's book. He didn't see the book.

"Can I help you, Darren?" asked Mr. Goggans.

"I'm looking for a red book with gold designs," Darren said. "It's called *My Travels to Other Dimensions.* It's by Sir Dagobert Ignatius LaFleur."

"Hmm," said Mr. Goggans. "I don't think I've heard of that one. Let me check the computer."

Mr. Goggans typed on his keyboard, then studied the computer screen, "Celia LaFleur, Martin LaFleur— no, nothing by Sir Dagobert LaFleur. Let me try the title." He typed again. "I'm sorry, Darren. It's not in the catalog."

"Thanks anyway," Darren said. *What happened to the book?* he wondered. *It was right there on the top shelf.* He sat down at a table and put his head in his hands.

Now he would never see all those other dimensions. He couldn't even go back to Floundermuffin to visit Thompson Erika.

Darren thought about groundermajigs and downingwings. He thought about the sail taxi, and then he thought about the downingwings again. *What if a kite had wings?* he wondered. *The wings could be connected to a tiny battery like the ones used for watches. The battery could move two long sticks attached to the wings.* Darren imagined big kites that looked like beautiful butterflies flapping their wings in the sky.

"Darren DeBakey!"

Darren looked up. Mr. Goggans was smiling at him. "It's time to go home, Darren."

"Thanks, Mr. Goggans," Darren said. He jumped up and raced out of the library. He couldn't wait to get to work on his next invention.